MILK

and

JUICE

A RECYCLING ROMANCE

Meredith Crandall Brown

HARPER

An Imprint of HarperCollinsPublishers

for my loves
Geoff, Abe & Zach

Milk and Juice: A Recycling Romance
Copyright © 2021 by Meredith Crandall Brown
All rights reserved. Manufactured in Italy. No part of this book may
be used or reproduced in any manner whatsoever without written permission
except in the case of brief quotations embodied in critical articles and reviews.
For information address HarperCollins Children's Books, a division of
HarperCollins Publishers, 195 Broadway, New York, NY 10007.
www.harpercollinschildrens.com

Library of Congress Control Number: 2020950473
ISBN 978-0-06-302185-3

Pages 18–19 languages in order from left to right: Mandarin, Spanish, Hindi,
Swahili, Japanese, Swedish, Russian, Italian, Creole, Maori, Balinese, Inupiat, Nepali,
Arabic, Yiddish, Tagalog, Navajo, Korean, Greek, French, Quechua, and Thai.

Meredith used her favorite graphite pencil and eraser, gouache,
watercolor pencils, Photoshop, laughter, and hard work to create
the illustrations for this book. Typography by Erica De Chavez.

21 22 23 24 25 RTLO 10 9 8 7 6 5 4 3 2 1
❖
First Edition

ONCE UPON A TIME, in a refrigerator not too far away, a jug of milk and a bottle of juice fell in love.

They enjoyed
daily adventures . . .

My Milk, you look *stunning* without your cap!

and kept each
other cold through
long, hot nights.

Then, one day, Juice was TAKEN AWAY.

All went dark for Juice,
and when it awoke–

. . . everything had changed.

Milk was nowhere to be found.

The cruel hand of fate kept returning.

Juice kept changing and Milk remained missing.

Eventually, Juice found itself in a basement.

Meanwhile, around the planet,
Milk searched for Juice.

Out of the dungeon,
but once again in a bin,
Juice fell into despair.

All went dark for Juice,

and when it awoke . . .

POP!

. . . Milk and Juice were together at last!

Or were they?

For darkness once again approached. . . .

NO! Not the darkness!
Stand back, cruel hand of
fate! For I am *JUICE* and
I WANT MY MILK!

Fate did not answer, but some stars appeared.

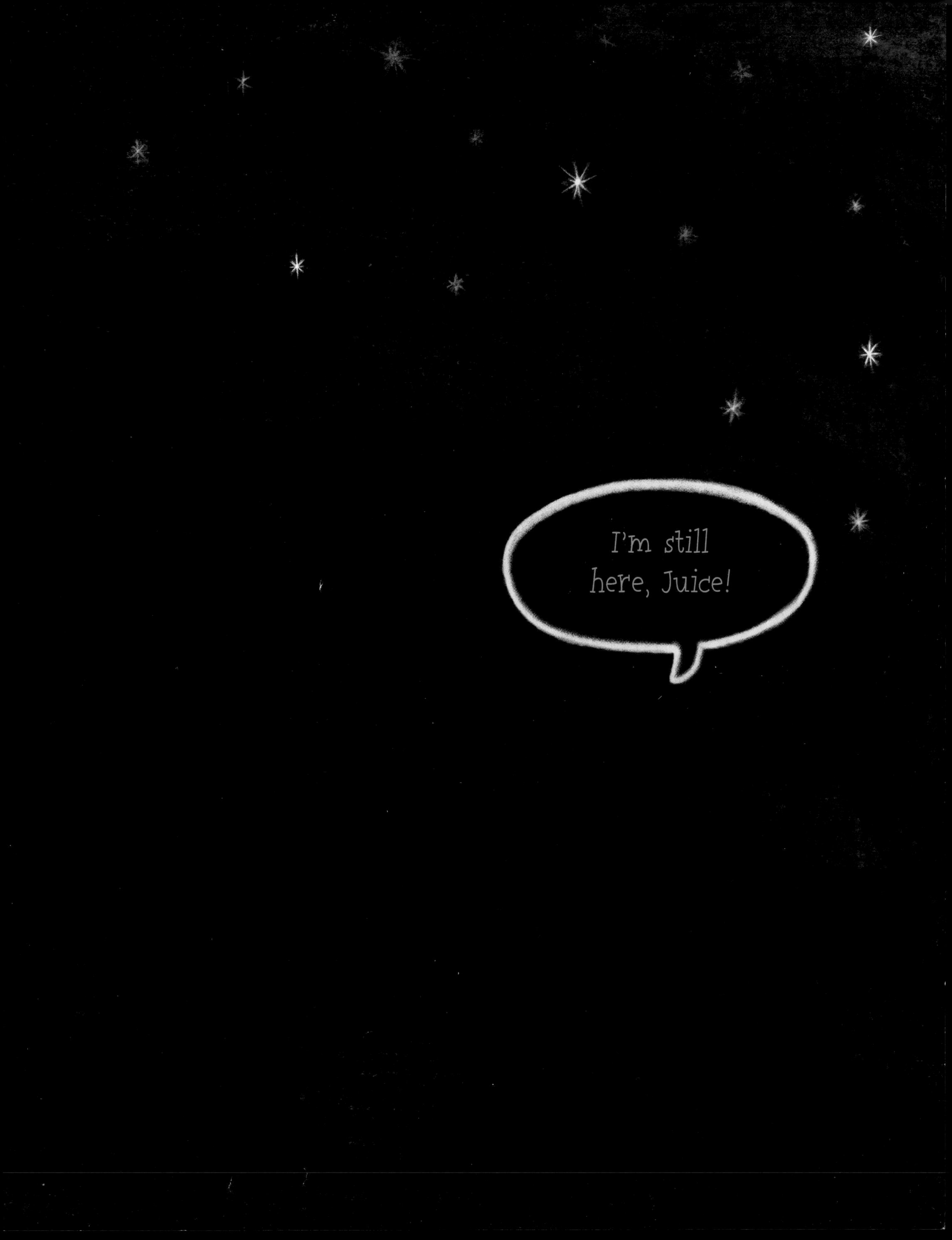
I'm still here, Juice!

Darkness came and went, but Milk and Juice were never again torn apart.

They lived happily ever after, *FOREVER* and *EVER.* . . .

WAIT! THE END?!

This can't be the end!!! I was on page four— I'M FAMOUS!

I feel deep down in my molecules that I'm DESTINED to become a toy pickup TRUCK!

I don't want it to end, either!

How will you become a pickup truck?

IT WILL HAPPEN LIKE THIS . . .

First, I'll need a shower.

THEN (don't look!),

CRUNCH!

I'll get flattened. (I'm okay!)

Next, I'll go in a bin to get . . .

collected and sent to a recycling plant.

At the recycling plant, I'll get . . .

SHREDDED!

(I'M OKAY!)

Boxed up . . .

and shipped to another plastics recycling plant.

→ (I'm on a boat!)

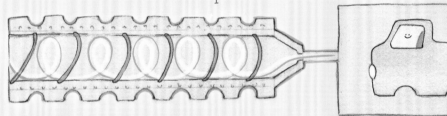

Where the hands of fate will heat me up in a rotating screw until I become liquid.

Then they will squirt me into a mold . . .

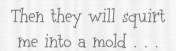

where I will harden and . . .

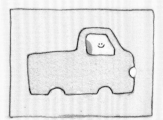

be assembled into my destiny . . .

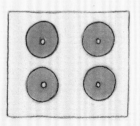